W9-DDJ-316

THE TROUBLE WITH WISHES

Here are some other Redfeather Books by Susan Beth Pfeffer

The Riddle Streak
Illustrated by Michael Chesworth

Sara Kate Saves the World
Illustrated by Tony DeLuna

Sara Kate, Superkid
Illustrated by Suzanne Hankins

Twin Surprises
Illustrated by Abby Carter

Twin Troubles
Illustrated by Abby Carter

SUSAN BETH PFEFFER

THE TROUBLE WITH WISHES

Illustrated by JENNIFER PLECAS

A Redfeather Book

HENRY HOLT AND COMPANY · NEW YORK

For B. P.

—J. P.

Henry Holt and Company, Inc.
Publishers since 1866
115 West 18th Street
New York, New York 10011

Henry Holt is a registered trademark of Henry Holt and Company, Inc.

Published in Canada by Fitzhenry & Whiteside Ltd.,
195 Allstate Parkway, Markham, Ontario L3R 4T8.

Library of Congress Cataloging-in-Publication Data
Pfeffer, Susan Beth. The trouble with wishes / by Susan Pfeffer;
illustrated by Jennifer Plecas.
p.   cm.—(A Redfeather Book)
Summary: Katie really wants to be the star of her third-grade class, but the noisy,
mean atmosphere of her class makes it hard to decide how to use the three wishes
given to her by an old magic lamp.
[1. Schools—Fiction.   2. Wishes—Fiction.   3. Behavior—Fiction.]
I. Plecas, Jennifer, ill.   II. Title.   III. Series: Redfeather Books.
PZ7.P44855To   1996   [Fic]—dc20   95-38200

ISBN 0-8050-3826-4

First Edition—1996

Printed in the United States of America on acid-free paper. ∞

1   3   5   7   9   10   8   6   4   2

Contents

THE TROUBLE WITH WISHES

1

A Normal Day in Katie Logan's Class

It was a normal day in Katie Logan's class.

Jeremy was pulling Jessica's hair. Michelle was hitting Roger. Kevin and David were competing to see who had better aim with spitballs. Amy and Lauren were going *tap-tap-tap* with their pens, seeing who could tap faster. Leslie was breaking a pencil and tossing the pieces at the kids sitting nearest her. And Michael was trying to bite people's necks.

The rest of the kids were trying to do their work. But it was hard with all that going on. Katie was working on a story she was writing. Ms. Bauman had told them to write a story about the thing they wanted most. Katie wasn't sure what she wanted most. There were so many things: video games, a horse, a baby sister, a thirty-five-inch TV set in her bedroom, a chance to star in the class play. She wasn't sure which would be the best to put into her story. Ms. Bauman probably wouldn't be too excited about the thirty-five-inch TV set, though.

"Class! Class!" Ms. Bauman shouted.

Katie sighed. Ms. Bauman spent a lot of her time shouting at the class, and it never seemed to make much difference.

"I want quiet, and I want it right now!" Ms. Bauman yelled.

The kids who were quiet stayed quiet. The rest kept making lots and lots of noise.

"Michael, I want you to sit down right now," Ms. Bauman ordered. "Leslie, I want you to stand up. Stop those spitballs this very minute, Kevin and David. Jeremy and Michelle, I want you to stand in

the back of the room. Lauren, go back to your seat this very minute. And Amy, go stand where Lauren was. Do you hear me? Do that right now!"

Things got even crazier then. Michael went to the back of the room along with Jeremy. Michelle took Kevin's chair. Amy started hitting Michael. Lauren went back to her chair but kept tapping. And Leslie stood up and began crying.

"Quiet!" Ms. Bauman screamed. "QUIET!"

The last scream worked. It usually did, at least for a few minutes. Then, Katie knew, everybody would get crazy again. They always did.

"I want all of us to be quiet for a minute," Ms. Bauman said. "And then I'm going to ask you all a question."

Katie wondered what the question was going to be. If it was multiplication, she was in trouble. She could never remember what seven times eight was.

"All right, class, here's my question," Ms. Bauman

said. "Do any of you know why you always behave this way?"

"What way?" Michelle asked.

"Why you're always so noisy and mean," Ms. Bauman said. "Other classes aren't like that. Students in other classes get along with each other. I've been teaching for ten years now and I've never seen a group of kids who fight as much as you do. Do you have any idea why?"

"I have to bite people," Michael piped up. "I'm a vampire."

Some of the kids laughed. Katie was surprised to see that not all of them thought he was funny.

"Michael, please," Ms. Bauman said. "I'm serious. I really want to know why this class behaves this way. It's November and we have a long way to go. At this rate, you kids aren't going to learn anything the whole school year. It's impossible to learn with so much noise. And I really want to know why you act this way because I want to see if I can change it and make this a happier classroom. Does anyone have any ideas?"

Katie thought about it. It would be nice if her class were quieter. Last year, in second grade, everybody got along, and they had learned a lot and had fun doing it. But there seemed to be something about this third-grade class that made everyone loud and crazy.

"No ideas?" Ms. Bauman said. "Nobody knows why so many of you are wasting our time screaming and making trouble?"

Jessica raised her hand. "I think it's because we don't like each other," she said. "If we liked each other, we wouldn't want to hit and get into fights and scream. We'd want to work together so we could learn more."

Katie rolled her eyes. Jessica was Little Miss Perfect. You could count on her to say just what Ms. Bauman wanted to hear.

And sure enough, she had. "I think you're right,

Jessica," Ms. Bauman said. "I think maybe we don't like each other. And just maybe if we were nicer, we would like each other, and this school year could be a good one after all."

But it was hard for Katie to hear what Ms. Bauman had said. Michelle was hitting Leslie. Roger and Amy were throwing pencil parts at each other. And Michael was trying to bite Kevin's neck.

Just a normal day in Katie's class.

2

The Talking Tree

"All right class," Ms. Bauman announced that afternoon. "Let's rehearse our play. Tomorrow we give our performance in front of the whole school. Are we ready?"

Katie noticed the class was quieter than it had been all day. They liked being in a play enough to stop causing trouble.

"I want the Native Americans in this corner," Ms. Bauman said. "Pilgrims, over here by me. And the nature kids, you stand by the desk. That's right. In the center."

Katie moved over to the desk area. Most of the kids were either Native Americans or Pilgrims. But she and three other kids played parts of nature. Katie was a tree. She hated being a tree.

What she really wanted was Jessica's part. Jessica, naturally enough, was the star of the show. She played the main Native American, the one who showed the Pilgrims about the ways of her people. She got to suggest they all have Thanksgiving dinner together. And she spoke the last line of the play. "Whatever the future may bring, may we all share our love for the harmony of the land and the seasons."

Ms. Bauman had explained that line to the class. Things hadn't been good for the Native Americans after Europeans got to the New World. Many had died of disease, and later on the settlers killed thousands of them and took away their land. And lots of times, Americans hadn't been good to the land either. They'd polluted it and littered it and turned something beautiful into something ugly.

"When Jessica says that line, I want all the grown-ups watching the play to think about those things," Ms. Bauman had told the class. "That's what makes this play special, and not just an ordinary Thanksgiving play. This play has depth."

Katie wasn't sure what depth was, but she knew Jessica had the most lines. Every kid in the class had at least one line to say. But only Katie was stuck being a tree.

"Now Jessica, show the Pilgrims the nature kids," Ms. Bauman said. "And nature kids, say your lines nice and loud. Remember you're going to be doing this play in front of the whole school tomorrow."

"We are people of the earth," Jessica said. "We love the gifts of nature. See what we love so deeply." She raised her hand and gestured toward the nature kids.

"I am the sun," Amy said. "I cast warmth and light upon the earth."

"I am the rain," Roger said. "I bring water to all the living things."

"I am a squirrel," Kevin said. "I am the nuts. I mean I eat the nuts."

The other kids laughed. When Ms. Bauman shushed them, they stopped.

Katie stood very still. She was supposed to go before Kevin, but Kevin was always jumping in and saying his line first.

"Katie," Ms. Bauman said, "don't you know your line yet?"

"I know it," Katie grumbled.

"Then say it nice and loud," Ms. Bauman said. "You go before Kevin, you know."

"I know," Katie said. If she were the star instead of Jessica, she'd say all her lines on time and nice and loud too. But she hated being a tree.

"I am the tree," Katie mumbled.

"Louder, Katie," Ms. Bauman said. "Let everyone in the audience know how important trees are."

"I am the tree," Katie shouted. "I am a home to the birds and the insects and the squirrels."

"Now Kevin," Ms. Bauman said.

"I am a squirrel," Kevin said. "I eat the nuts."

"The sun, the rain, the tree, the squirrel," Jessica said, pointing at each one as she spoke. "They are nature's gifts to us, her grateful children."

"And we are grateful too," Danny said. He was First Pilgrim, the second-best part. "How can we show our gratitude, O Wise Woman?"

"Let us have a festival of thanks," Jessica said. "A day for giving thanks for all of nature's gifts."

Katie stopped listening after that. She had nothing more to do. One line, all about how great it was to be a tree, and that was it. Jessica had twenty-three lines. Katie knew because she'd counted. Twenty-three lines and all the other kids calling her a wise woman.

It was enough to make Katie sick. No wonder her classmates didn't like each other. Not with teacher's pets like Jessica around getting all the best stuff while everyone else was stuck being dumb things like trees.

3

The Talking Litter

After school that day, Katie decided to walk home through the park.

She didn't know why. She almost never walked that way. Usually she walked with the other kids past the middle school, where her big brother, Alex, was a student. Sometimes she'd run into Alex and they'd walk home together.

But that day Katie just felt like walking through the park. She figured it was because there were so many trees there. If she was going to be a tree, she might as well spend some time with them.

When Katie was in the park, she always got on the swings, since they were her favorite, but today she decided to skip them. Instead she walked on one of the paths and stared at trees. Katie liked trees. She just didn't want to be one.

When she was nearly home, Katie noticed a big cereal box on the ground. It was a strange thing to see in a park, but there it was. She could see it had been there for a while. It had rained a couple of days before, and the box was kind of squishy.

Katie wondered what to do. Everybody else had left the box. Maybe she should too.

But then she remembered what Ms. Bauman had said about how Americans had littered the country. And Katie knew there was a big garbage can at the end of the path. It wouldn't hurt to pick up the box and throw it away. And it would help the earth and make it a prettier place.

Katie bent down and picked up the box. It felt soggy and weird. She didn't like it at all, but she held on to it and carried it to the garbage can.

As she was getting ready to throw the box away, something happened. The cereal box turned into something metal and heavy. It looked kind of like a watering can.

Katie dropped it and screamed. She didn't care for wet yucky things turning into heavy metal.

"Pick me up."

Katie wasn't sure, but it sounded like a voice was coming from what used to be the cereal box.

"Pick me up."

Katie bent down and picked up the metal thing. Maybe it was a space alien. If she were the first person to discover a space alien, she'd be on TV, and then maybe her parents would buy her a thirty-five-inch set for her room.

"For years I have rested on the forest ground," the metal thing said. "I have taken many forms over the years. I have been injured birds, broken branches, and most recently, I have been litter."

"Are you a space alien?" Katie asked.

"I am not a space alien," the metal thing replied. "I am a magic lamp."

"You don't look like a lamp," Katie said, hoping nobody would notice she was talking to something metal. "Where's your lightbulb?"

"I was a lamp before the invention of lightbulbs," the lamp explained. "I was a lamp before Thomas Edison invented electric lights."

"I thought you were a cereal box," Katie said.

"I took that form to find a person to reward," the lamp said. "You alone have proven worthy of my great gift."

"You're giving me something?" Katie asked. First she got excited, and then she remembered all the lessons she'd been taught about taking things from strangers. "I'm sorry," she said. "But I can't take anything from you."

"I'm not going to give you candy," the lamp said. "I am a magic lamp, not a kidnapper."

"I don't know," Katie said.

"I am going to give you the greatest gift a lamp can offer," the lamp said. "You will have three wishes granted to you. Anything you wish for will be yours."

"Really?" Katie exclaimed. "You mean like if I wished for a thirty-five-inch TV set for my bedroom, I'd get it?"

"Yes," the lamp replied. "Although I had hoped someone as worthy as you might first think about wishing for world peace."

"I'll wish for that second," Katie said. "I promise."

"Promise me nothing," the lamp said. "Except that you will think very carefully about what you wish for and why. A gift such as mine should not be taken lightly."

"Okay," Katie agreed, although it seemed to her that between the TV set and world peace, she only had one wish left and that wasn't so much.

"Think before you wish," the lamp said, and then it disappeared.

Katie screamed again. But then she decided the lamp had simply gotten beamed up to a starship somewhere. She didn't care where it had gone. She had three wishes to call her own.

4

The Trick with Wishes

By the time Katie got home, she wasn't sure she wanted to throw her first wish away on a TV set. If she wished to be incredibly rich, then she could buy as many TV sets as she wanted. Why settle for just one?

World peace was probably a good idea, although Katie wasn't sure what that would get her. Still, if she were incredibly rich, she supposed she could give away a wish to make the world a happier place.

It was that third wish that was tricky. Maybe she should be beautiful. Maybe she should be a princess.

Maybe she should be the smartest person in the world. It seemed awfully unfair that there were so many great things to wish for and she was entitled to only three of them.

Alex was already home when Katie arrived. He was lying on the sofa playing with the remote control.

"I have three wishes," Katie announced.

"What are you talking about?" Alex asked.

Katie paused for a moment. "For homework," she said. "I have three wishes to write about for homework. If you had three wishes, what would they be?"

"Wishes are tricky," Alex said. He hit the mute button, then left the TV on C-Span. "I read this story once about this guy who got three wishes and he wished for stuff you'd think was good, like being rich, but everything he wished for turned out bad. Scary. You wouldn't like the story."

Katie nodded. Her class on a really bad day was scary enough for her. "But if you only wish for good stuff, it can't turn out bad," she protested. "Like just suppose I wished for a thirty-five-inch TV set for my bedroom. How could that turn out bad?"

Alex thought about it. "You might get a TV set that doesn't work," he said. "Or maybe you get the TV but no cable hookup, so all you get are four stations. Or maybe the money for the TV comes from insurance on some kind of awful accident. Or you get the TV and somebody breaks into the house and steals it. Or maybe the TV's wiring is screwed up and it starts an electrical fire. Lots of bad stuff could happen."

Katie didn't like any of this. But she especially didn't like the part about the electricity. Her magic lamp said it came from before electricity was invented. It might not know how to handle a thirty-five-inch TV set.

"Okay," she said. "So I don't wish for a TV. I could wish to be incredibly rich instead."

"That's what happened in the story," Alex said. "The guy wished to be rich, and the way he became rich was his son was killed and he got the insurance. You don't want Dad or Mom to get killed just so you could be rich, do you?"

"Of course not," Katie said. "Isn't there some other way I could get rich?"

"I don't know," Alex said. "You have to be eighteen to buy a lottery ticket. I guess maybe you could get rich because it turns out you're not really Katie Logan. I mean maybe you were switched at birth and you're really some rich kid and some rich kid is really Katie Logan. But then you'd have to move away and live with a family you don't know. That could happen, I guess."

Dad always made Katie do her homework before she could watch TV, and Mom was always after her to keep her room straight, and Alex could be a big tease sometimes. But they were Katie's family, and she didn't like the idea of having to leave them and live with some rich strangers.

"Okay, so I wouldn't wish to be rich or have a TV

set," she said, although those had been her two favorite wishes and she was sorry to see them go. "What about world peace? I could wish for world peace. What would be wrong with that?"

"I'm not sure," Alex said. "We've never had world peace."

"That's because no one ever wished for it," Katie said. No one with a magic lamp, she added to herself.

"World peace sounds okay," Alex said. "It sounds pretty safe. But maybe it's not such a good idea."

"Why not?" Katie asked. She hoped Alex could come up with some good reasons, so she wouldn't have to waste a wish on it.

"Well suppose there's world peace," Alex said. "And nobody dies in wars anymore. Then maybe there'd be too many people on Earth and not enough food, and we'd all die from hunger."

"That would be terrible," Katie gasped. She hated

the idea that she would be responsible for every-body's going hungry.

"And some good stuff comes from wars," Alex said. "Inventions and medicines and stuff like that. Or suppose somebody really bad like Hitler came into power and there was world peace so he got to stay in power and kill people and nobody stopped him. That wouldn't be good either."

Hitler and hunger and all her fault.

"So what would you do if you had three wishes?" Katie asked. She had them, after all. She might as well get some use out of them.

"I don't know," Alex said. "But I'd sure be careful what I wished for."

5

How to Be a Star in One Easy Wish

Katie spent that evening making lists of all the different things she could wish for and all the ways those wishes could turn out wrong. It drove her crazy. If she were rich, she'd be unhappy with the way she got to be rich. If she were supersmart, she'd be taken away from her family and made to think all the time to come up with answers to the world's problems. If she were a princess, then she'd have to live in a country with kings and queens, and she couldn't even be an American. If she were beautiful, then she'd probably become a model and stand around getting her picture taken all the time.

Actually, being beautiful didn't sound that bad. It might be fun being a model, and then she could earn lots of money and buy a TV set—one that worked and didn't cause fires. Beauty was definitely a possibility, until Katie started wondering how she'd get to be beautiful. The only way she could come up with was she'd have to be in a horrible accident and they'd have to do lots and lots of plastic surgery on her and when it was all done she would look beautiful but wouldn't look anything like herself. That didn't sound so great either.

Finally Katie put away her list and stared at her times tables instead. She almost wished she could memorize those stupid eights that were giving her so much trouble, until she realized what a waste of a wish that would be.

Three wishes were a lot of bother. Next time she'd

just leave the litter where she found it. Let the earth take care of itself.

Katie sat straight up. That was it. She'd wish for Jessica's part in the play. It was perfect. If she had only one wish, she might not waste it on that. But she'd still have two wishes to go, so she might as well use one to get something she really wanted.

She almost wished for it right away, but then she stopped herself. Suppose she wished for Jessica's part and went to school the next day and found out Jessica had been hit by a car? She wouldn't have to die or anything, just be injured enough to miss school. But Katie would feel terrible. Sure Jessica was Little Miss Perfect and Katie couldn't stand her. But she didn't want to be responsible for her being hit by a car. And Katie didn't know what the lamp would do. Maybe it would kill Jessica. Katie wasn't about to take any chances.

And if something really awful happened to Jessica, then Katie would have to wish that away to make her come back to life, and she'd be down to her

last wish. Not to mention the fact that if Katie got Jessica's part knowing Jessica was in an accident and it was all her fault, she wouldn't enjoy playing the wise Native American woman. So she wouldn't have anything to show for her two wishes except a guilty conscience.

Still, the idea of starring in the play appealed to Katie. She knew it was the right thing to wish for. It was just a case of wishing for it the right way.

Alex would know, she decided. She left her bedroom and went to his. Alex was at his desk, doing his homework.

"I still have these three wishes," Katie said. "And it seemed to me I'd like to be the star of my class play tomorrow. I was trying to figure out how to wish for it and not get Jessica hit by a car or something."

"I think you have to take some chances with three wishes," Alex said. "If you wish for it while you're at school, Jessica won't get hit by a car there. After all, you're not wishing for something bad to happen to her, just for something good to happen to you."

"Exactly," Katie said. "So you think it would be safe for me to wish to be the star, just as long as I do it when Jessica can't get hit by a car." She giggled. "That's a poem."

"I think it would be okay," Alex said. "Is Jessica going to read this composition?"

"What composition?" Katie asked. "Oh, you mean the one I'm working on about the three wishes."

"I don't think I'd like it if I knew someone was wishing for my part," Alex said.

"Jessica won't mind," Katie said. "She won't know what happened. I mean, Ms. Bauman said we didn't have to read our compositions out loud. She said wishes are private."

"Then that's what I'd do," Alex said. "I'd wish for the starring role when I was sure Jessica couldn't get hurt."

"That's what I'll do then," Katie said. "I'll get to be the star and I'll still have two wishes left!"

6

A Star Isn't Born

"Now class," Ms. Bauman said, as Katie's class waited for all the kids in the school to finish piling into the auditorium. "I want all of you to stand up straight and say your lines nice and loud. Everyone remember his or her place?"

"Yes, Ms. Bauman," the class replied.

Their teacher smiled at them. "You're going to be great," she said. "Now go out there and do yourselves proud."

This is it, Katie told herself. She closed her eyes, the way she would if she were blowing out birthday candles, and whispered, "I wish I was the star of the play."

Instantly, Jessica began coughing. Ms. Bauman ran to her side. "Are you all right?" she asked.

Jessica coughed some more and then looked up at Ms. Bauman. "I've lost my voice," she whispered.

Katie sure hoped it wasn't permanent. If it was, she was going to have to waste a wish getting Jessica's voice back.

"Can you play your part?" Ms. Bauman asked.

Jessica shook her head.

"I can do it," Katie offered. "Let me, please."

"All right, Katie," Ms. Bauman said. "Jessica, I want you to go to the nurse's office right away. Katie, you're going out there a nobody. I expect you to come back a star."

Katie didn't exactly think of herself as a nobody, but she nodded anyway and raced onto the stage. Or at least she raced as fast as she could dressed up like a tree.

"We are Pilgrims in a new land," Danny said.

"We have come here to make our home," Lauren said. "A home where we can practice our religion under free skies."

"I am frightened, Mother," Leslie said. She got the child's part because she was the shortest kid in the class. "This land looks nothing like England."

"England was our home before," Michael said. "But now we are in Plymouth Colony, our new home."

"Perhaps someone will befriend us," Danny said.

That was the cue for the wise woman. Katie inched herself forward on the stage. "I will help you, my new friends," she said.

The Pilgrims stared at her.

"I am a Native American woman," Katie said. "My name in your language means Gift of Nature."

"You don't look like a Native American woman," Leslie said. "You look like a tree."

The audience laughed.

"I never heard a tree talk before," Danny said.

Katie looked down and realized that even though she had Jessica's part, she was still dressed like a tree.

"I know I'm a tree," she said, making up the lines as she went along. "I'm a wise Native American tree," Katie said. She hoped the other kids would realize she was also playing the wise Native American woman.

"We are people of the earth," Katie said. "We love the gifts of nature. See what we love so deeply." She tried to gesture the way Jessica always did, but her arms were by her side in the tree costume. She bent her head sideways instead, so it looked like the treetop was swaying.

"Should I say my line?" Amy asked, so loud the entire audience could hear her. That only made them laugh louder.

"Yes, yes," Ms. Bauman whispered from offstage. "Just go on with your line."

"I am the sun," Amy said. "I . . . I . . . I forget!"

"I cast warmth and light upon the earth," Katie said. If she was going to say the wise woman's lines, she might as well say the sun's lines as well.

"You don't cast light," Leslie said. "You're a tree. You cast shade."

"I'm just trying to help," Katie told her. But Leslie was laughing too hard to listen.

"I am the rain," Roger said, just like he was supposed to. "I bring water to all living things."

"I am a squirrel," Kevin said, jumping ahead of Katie's line the way he always did. "And I'm not the only nut in this place. I mean I eat only nuts in this place."

The audience howled.

"I am the tree," Katie said, ignoring the audience's hysteria. "I am a home to the birds and the insects and the squirrels." She stood still, hoping that people would calm down, until she realized the next line was Jessica's and she had to say it too.

"The sun, the rain, the tree, the squirrel," Katie

said. She knew the wise Native American woman was supposed to point at each one of them. She bent her head a little, then a little more, and a little more, until she lost her balance and toppled to the ground.

"Somebody help me get up," Katie whispered, but nobody did. The rest of the cast just stared at her lying on the stage.

Katie knew she was the star, and it was up to her to keep the show going. "Let us have a festival of thanks," she shouted. "A day for giving thanks for all of nature's gifts."

All the other kids, the ones playing Native Americans and Pilgrims, raced up onto the stage. "Oh yes, oh yes," they all said. "A festival of thanks for nature's gifts." Two of them tripped over Katie and fell smack onto the floor.

After that, everybody got crazy. Leslie began hitting Roger. Kevin and David wrestled with each other. And Michael shouted that he was a Pilgrim vampire and ran around trying to bite everybody's neck.

"Class, class!" Ms. Bauman yelled. She raced onto the stage and began pushing the kids off. The kids in the audience were yelling and screaming as well, and their teachers were shouting at them.

Katie kept trying to stand up, knowing it was all her fault. "I wish I was just a—" she began, but then stopped herself. She had almost wished she were just a tree, and for all she knew, that would have made her a real tree forever. Instead she began to cry.

"Look at that," David said, pointing at her. "She's turned into a weeping willow!"

But Katie was crying too hard even to care.

☆ 7. ☆

Another Wish Gone

It took a while for them to get back into their classroom, and even longer before they had calmed down enough to sit in their chairs. When they finally did, Jessica returned. "I still can't talk," she whispered. "The nurse doesn't know why."

Katie gritted her teeth. "I wish Jessica could talk again," she muttered.

"I can talk again!" Jessica exclaimed. "My voice is back."

"Well that's one good thing," Ms. Bauman said.

"Class, I want to congratulate you. You turned a little difficulty into a full-fledged riot."

"It wasn't our fault," Lauren protested. "Nobody told us the wise woman was going to be a tree."

"I thought Katie just stole the part," Michael said. "She's been telling everybody how much she wants it and how unfair it is she has to be a tree."

"I bet she made Jessica start coughing," Leslie said. "Just so she could be the star."

"Now class, stop it," Ms. Bauman scolded. "Katie doesn't have magic powers. She didn't do anything except offer to take over Jessica's role when Jessica lost her voice."

"I didn't want it to turn out this way," Katie sobbed. "I wanted the play to be a big success."

"I don't know," Leslie said. "I still think Katie must have done something to Jessica."

"Katie did nothing to Jessica," Ms. Bauman said. "And it wasn't Katie's fault you all started acting up.

Katie didn't make the rest of you say those funny lines. And she certainly didn't make Michael do his vampire act."

"But it was funny when she started talking like that," Danny said. "Pretending she was the wise woman when she was dressed up like a tree."

"When a tree starts telling you it's a wise woman, you sort of have to say something," Leslie said. "Otherwise you're the one who's going to look stupid, and not the stupid tree."

"And I am a vampire," Michael said. "I must drink people's blood."

Everybody laughed. Everybody except Katie and Ms. Bauman.

"I'm sorry," Ms. Bauman said. "All this was my fault."

For a moment the class was quiet. The kids weren't used to a grown-up apologizing to them.

"I was so excited about the play and how good you were in it, I forgot what you children are really

like," Ms. Bauman said. "I forgot you can't be trusted to cooperate. I forgot you have to be told every single thing you must do, that you can't figure things out for yourselves. I forgot you aren't like third-graders should be. You're more like babies, and babies just can't be trusted on a stage. Just because you were so good in your play, I forgot how much, as Jessica said the other day, you don't like each other. Katie was very brave offering to take over Jessica's part. Without someone saying the wise woman's lines, there is no play. And Katie knew all those lines, just the way an understudy would. You're right. She did look silly dressed like a tree, but she tried to cover that and you wouldn't let her. And now, instead of taking responsibility for yourselves, you're blaming this whole mess on Katie. You should all be ashamed of yourselves. All of you, except Katie and Jessica."

"The play was good until Katie messed it up," Leslie said.

"Yes, it was," Amy cried. "Everything that happened was all Katie's fault."

"It sure was," the class said. "It was Katie's fault."

"Class, stop it," Ms. Bauman said, but Katie didn't care. The problem was she knew the class was right and Ms. Bauman was wrong. It was all her fault, and she was going to have to live with that for the rest of her life.

She was also going to have to live with the third wish. And whatever she wished for was going to have to work on the first try, because there'd be no fourth wish to correct mistakes.

8

The Trick with Times Tables

It was a normal day in Katie Logan's class.

Jeremy was pulling Jessica's hair. Michelle was hitting Kevin. David and Roger were competing to see who had better aim with spitballs. Amy and Lauren were tapping on each other's desks with their pens. Leslie was tossing broken crayons at the kids sitting nearest her. And Michael was trying to bite people's necks.

The rest of the kids had given up trying to do their work. Half of them were fighting. The other half, including Katie, just sat there watching.

Ms. Bauman stood in front of the class shouting at them, but nobody heard her—or if they did, they didn't pay any attention. Finally Ms. Bauman screamed, "I WISH YOU WOULD ALL DISAPPEAR!"

Katie gasped. What if Ms. Bauman had three wishes? How long would it take before none of them existed?

But it seemed Ms. Bauman didn't have that kind of power. All the kids kept on doing what they'd been doing the instant before she screamed.

Katie looked around her and sighed. She used to like the kids in her class, most of them anyway. They'd gotten along pretty well in second grade. At least they weren't all crazy the way they seemed to be nowadays.

Ms. Bauman looked about ready to cry. Katie felt bad for her. It must be awful trying to teach kids who were always hitting each other or biting or screaming.

Katie tried to think what Ms. Bauman would really wish for if she had just one wish left. She'd probably read the same scary story Alex had and wouldn't risk wishing for lots of money or even great beauty. And Katie liked to think she wouldn't wish that all of them would disappear either. Ms. Bauman liked Jessica and Danny. Katie had the feeling Ms. Bauman liked her too, most of the time.

Would she wish that they were all quiet? Katie sure hoped not. What if they all lost their voices, the way Jessica had? No, that wish was too risky also.

"Stop pulling my hair!" Jessica shouted. "You're a stupid idiot, Jeremy, and I hate you!"

Katie was shocked. Jessica never talked like that. Maybe it was because she was disappointed she hadn't gotten to play the wise woman. Katie hadn't thought before about how that must have made Jessica feel. She'd been as mean to Jessica as Jeremy was, but Jessica didn't know it. She'd messed up the class play, the one thing they all had liked working on together, and nobody knew it. If she hadn't been so greedy, the class would have finally had something to be proud of. Instead the bad kids stayed bad, and now even the good kids like Jessica were acting up.

Katie knew she was going to have to give up her third wish. She owed it to Jessica, to Ms. Bauman, to her whole class. This last wish was giving her a headache anyway, worrying that whatever she wished would turn out bad. And she'd lived this long without a thirty-five-inch TV set in her bedroom. She supposed she could wait a little longer.

"I wish we all liked each other," she whispered.

Suddenly, the class was quiet. Jeremy stopped pulling Jessica's hair. Michelle stopped hitting Kevin. David and Roger stopped tossing spitballs. Amy and Lauren stopped tapping each other's desks. Leslie stopped throwing crayons at the kids sitting nearest her. And Michael stopped biting people's necks.

"Now class," Ms. Bauman said. "Let's get back to our seats and practice our times tables."

And they all did. Katie watched in amazement as the class settled down and began working.

"Who knows their sevens?" Ms. Bauman asked. "Katie, what is seven times eight?"

Katie couldn't believe it. She'd given up her last best wish only to be stuck with seven times eight. "Fifty-four?" she tried. She knew fifty-four was something times something.

"Is that right, class?" Ms. Bauman asked.

"No, Ms. Bauman," the class said.

"Who knows the right answer?" Ms. Bauman asked.

"I do," Leslie said. "Seven times eight is fifty-six."

"That's right, Leslie," Ms. Bauman said.

"Can I teach Katie my trick for remembering?" Leslie said. "I used to have trouble with seven times eight until I learned the trick."

"Let's hear your trick, Leslie," Ms. Bauman said.

"I go five-six-seven-eight," Leslie said. "Seven times eight is five-six. Fifty-six. It works for me. I hope it'll work for you too, Katie."

David raised his hand. "I have trouble with seven

times eight also," he said. "Thank you, Leslie, for teaching me that trick."

"Yes, thank you," Katie said. She couldn't believe it. A minute before, the class had been hitting and screaming. And now they were raising their hands to say thank you.

And Katie really liked Leslie for teaching her the trick. She liked David for admitting he had trouble with seven times eight. As a matter of fact, Katie liked just about everybody in her class just then.

And that felt so good, it was worth a wish.

9

When Wishes Come True

It was another normal day in Katie Logan's class.

In one corner, ten of the kids were reading out loud to each other the stories they'd written on the thing they wanted most. In another section of the room, some of the kids were going over their times tables. A few of the kids were sitting by Ms. Bauman's desk while she gave them individual help with their reading. And in the back of the room, some of the kids were putting together a display about the life of early settlers in America.

Nobody was shouting, crying, tapping, or throwing things. Instead they were helping each other learn and enjoying every minute of it.

After a while, Ms. Bauman told them to go back to their regular chairs. All the kids did. Nobody kicked anyone on his or her way back. When Michael brushed against Leslie, he even said he was sorry. And Leslie didn't start crying.

"Now class, I have some very good news for you," Ms. Bauman said. "I hope you'll be as excited as I am."

"What is it, Ms. Bauman?" the class asked

"I spoke to the principal about our class play," Ms. Bauman said. "I told him how Jessica had lost her voice at the last minute, and how Katie had volunteered to take her part, but we didn't have a chance to warn any of the rest of you."

"That was pretty funny," Danny said.

The rest of the class laughed. But it wasn't a mean laugh.

"The principal was very sympathetic," Ms. Bauman said. "She said she was once in a play when the main actor forgot all his lines, and the rest of the actors had to go on with the play anyway. She said she'd really like to see what our play would be like when it's done the right way, the way we'd rehearsed it."

Michelle raised her hand. "Does that mean we can do the play again?" she asked.

"You're absolutely right, Michelle," Ms. Bauman said. "The principal said we could do our play Friday afternoon. That gives us three days to rehearse it again. How does that sound to you, class? Do you like the idea of putting on the play just the way it should be?"

"Yay!" the class shouted.

Jessica raised her hand. "Ms. Bauman, could we change something in the play?" she asked.

"What do you think should be changed?" Ms. Bauman asked.

"Could the tree have some of the wise woman's lines?" Jessica asked. "I bet Katie could say them real well if she had the chance. And nobody would laugh if they knew she was going to say them. After all, she was always going to be a talking tree."

"Katie, would you like that?" Ms. Bauman asked.

"Yes, please," Katie said. "I'd like that a lot."

"Very well," Ms. Bauman said. "During lunch today, I'll rewrite the play so the tree gets some more lines. Now let's get back to our science lesson."

At lunch that day, Katie went up to Jessica. "Thank you," she said, "for giving up some of your lines."

"You're welcome," Jessica said. "I wanted you to have them because you're so nice."

"I'm nice?" Katie asked.

"I think you're the nicest girl in the class," Jessica said. "When I lost my voice, I heard you wish that I'd get it back. Sometimes I think I might not have, if you hadn't wished for it. And I heard you wish we all liked each other too. That was what I had said, about how we didn't like each other and that's why we kept fighting. I don't know if your wish made a

difference, but I thought you were really nice to say it out loud that way. It meant you listened to what other people said and you cared about us all."

"Oh," Katie said.

"I'd like us to be friends," Jessica said. "Is that okay with you?"

"It's fine with me," Katie said, and then she smiled. "It's what I've always wished for."

"You know what I've always wished for?" Jessica asked.

"No, what?" Katie said.

"A twenty-seven-inch TV set for my bedroom," Jessica said. "Isn't that terrible?"

"It sure is," Katie said. "I always wished for a thirty-five-inch TV myself!"

And the two girls laughed and laughed.

BAKER & TAYLOR